THE EMPTY
QUARTER

THE EMPTY QUARTER

Stories

Sharon Mesmer

Hanging Loose Press
Brooklyn, New York

Published by Hanging Loose Press, 231 Wyckoff Street, Brooklyn, NY 11217-2208. All rights reserved. No part of this book may be reproduced without the publisher's written permission, except for brief quotations in reviews.

Printed in the United States of America
10 9 8 7 6 5 4 3 2 1

Hanging Loose Press thanks the Literature Program of the New York State Council on the Arts for a grant in support of the publication of this book. The author thanks the New York Foundation for the Arts for a fellowship which enabled her to complete this book.

Cover art and design by David Borchart

Photo of author by Toshiaki Takamura

ACKNOWLEDGMENTS

"As If" appeared in *Poets & Writers* and *Hanging Loose*; "Eleusis" in the anthology *Unbearables* (Autonomedia); "Misty" in *Breukelen*; "The Empty Quarter" in *Central Park*; "Eleusis" was previously published in *Half Angel, Half Lunch* (Hard Press) and "The Hours of a Transfigured Night" by Jordan Zinovich as part of the Alley Tracts series.

Many thanks to those who helped, whether they knew it or not: as always the staff of the MacDowell Colony, the staff of Hawthornden Castle, Bob Hershon, Larry Fagin, Robert Polito, Jackson Taylor, Scott Berry, Patricia Underwood, Jonathan Veitch, Lori Andiman, Ron Kolm, Joe Maynard, Tom Devaney, Mitch Highfill, Jim Feast, Barbara Paley-Israel, Ian Bascetta, Natalya Murakhver, Jon Gams, Michael Gizzi, Therese Eiben, Eileen Truszkowski, Edna Gendel, Ron Siegel, Ed Stone, the Minasola family, Marjorie Shaxted — and most especially Jewel Radtke.

Library of Congress Cataloging-in-Publication Data

Mesmer, Sharon.
    The empty quarter / Sharon Mesmer.
      p. cm.
    ISBN 1-882413-67-9 -- ISBN 1-882413-66-0 (pbk.)
       1. United States—Social life and customs—20th century—
      Fiction. I. Title
PS3563.E74628 E47   1999
813'.54--dc21   99-052164

Produced at The Print Center, Inc. 225 Varick St., New York, NY 10014, a non-profit facility for literary and arts-related publications. (212) 206-8465

University of Texas
at San Antonio

TABLE OF CONTENTS

For Mom, David, & Nicholas

Silver

"Those women are monsters! They'll eat you alive!"
Silver tore off the sequined dress.

"Those big blondes with their big tits and teeth!"

She stamped and kicked the dress away, then ran out of the room naked. The models looked down, shook their high heads and laughed.

I laughed the loudest. I was glad Silver felt bad. I was secretly in love with her and maybe she knew it, because she took every opportunity to humiliate me. Like the time she invited me to a restaurant: it's inexpensive, she said, don't dress up. But it was expensive, everyone was dressed up, and she whispered things about me to some guy she was with.

After the fashion show I masturbated while looking at a blonde on all fours in a men's magazine, wondering what Silver's retribution for my laughing would be.

But I beat her to it: I wrote her a letter, ending our friendship. I put in a line by Bob Dylan from "Just Like A Woman."

When I saw her again she smelled like a church and her eyes were wet. She said to forgive her, tear up the letter and then we'll have dinner.

I forgave her, tore up the letter. She reminded me of the sister I'd lost in the sewer.

I Married a Bay City Roller

You never dreamed I'd marry a Bay City Roller, did you, Marianne?

Remember when we went to the premiere of the documentary about them and that guy spilled coffee in your cuffs and you went to the bathroom to clean up and when you came back I wasn't in my seat and we never saw each other again? Well, would you believe that while you were in the bathroom I asked the guy sitting next to me to watch our seats while I went for popcorn and it turned out to be Alan, the bass player, the one we both liked because he looked like Eddie the stock boy from Goldblatt's? How did I know it was him? Well, who else who looked like Eddie, with a thick Scottish accent like that, would be sitting in a theatre on the bad side of Kankakee watching a Bay City Rollers documentary? Why was he even there? Do you think I thought to ask, after what he said to me first:

"Didja hear about the girl who married a mole?"

At least that's what I *thought* he said, so isn't it easy to see how I ended up making out with him behind the discount suede place two hours later? And can you believe the next day I was backstage at one of their concerts in Scotland, sitting there with fifteen life-size teddy bears with Bay City Roller faces and mountains of plaid M&Ms? Every night there were parties with different celebrities, and I met — are you sitting down, Marianne? — George and Alana Hamilton, Helen Reddy, Tony Orlando, Howard Cosell, the guy who played Gopher on "The Love Boat," Toni Tenille, Jimmy "J.J." Walker — need I say more? And if you're thinking all that was pretty incredible, Alan insisted I move to Glasgow and live with them in the big apartment they all shared — can't you just see me, the only girl, living with ALL the Bay City Rollers in Glasgow? Is it any wonder I disappeared for five years? Well, it wasn't really an apartment but one floor of an abandoned orphanage from the 1940's with no furniture and fluorescent department store lights that flickered all the time and gave some people seizures, and since there was no heat we used a toilet rigged up like a fireplace to burn wood, and plus this weird gas always leaked from the mattresses, and since we couldn't really do laundry (we had to go across the street to the gas station to get water) the pillows always had ear wax all over them — Scottish people have ear wax problems — but that was because their manager used up all their rent and food money on male prostitutes and ornamental goldfish — he was president of the International Live Breeders Club: how weird is that? And I bet you thought they were all clean and wholesome, right? Well, can you believe they were all heroin addicts, even Alan? I didn't care — that kind of thing always makes a rock star more appealing, right? But all of them together weren't as bad as that asshole Andy Gibb, who got them all started on drugs, but think about it, Marianne: wouldn't you choose mattress gas, pillow pizza and Andy Gibb's heroin over Aunt Ma and Uncle Pa in two rooms over the plastic plate factory on the bad side of Kankakee?

Are you mad that you never got a wedding invitation? Don't you think I'm mad because there weren't any? That there wasn't even a real wedding? Their manager messed it all up, and would you believe on our wedding day we ended up on a dock in the Firth of Forth with Alan getting his skull cracked open by drunken steeplejacks ? Is it any wonder he had all those mental problems? Plus, if you thought our childhoods were bad, would you believe his parents (they were disabled circus acrobats waiting for liver transplants) tried to make him spontaneously combust by feeding him haggis laced with gunpowder and forcing him to sleep in the stove? Can you really blame him for getting his father drunk and stuffing him in a gunny sack and running over him in a lorry? Doesn't that make the whole "Aunt Ma and Uncle Pa" thing tame by comparison? You're probably thinking I deserved all I got for marrying him, but don't you think if I knew all this stuff I wouldn't have married him in the first place? But I mean, you see a guy in a photo with Britt Eklund and you think you're going to have a certain kind of life, right?

Did you read in the paper about when he was forced to leave the group? Their manager had the bright idea that Alan was too old — he was only 25; can you believe that? And seeing as how the group was his and his brother Derek's idea in the first place, way back in 1971, how cruel is that? It really messed Alan up because he didn't want to live in the abandoned orphanage with the other Rollers anymore, so he just hung out down at the pub and got beaten up all the time — guys used to want to fight him because he was a famous teen idol, and if you were a forty-five year old alcoholic one-eyed unemployed stevedore supporting eleven demented kids and a mean wife by fixing radiators in the summer, wouldn't you hate a teen idol? When he started coming home and taking it out on me I figured it was time for a change so I got a job giving out sausage samples at the Safeway and with the money I made I found us our own apartment, and at the same time suggested Alan get interested in a hobby because he was getting jealous of the freedom my sausage sample job gave me, but the only thing he wanted to take up was fencing, and would you trust someone like Alan with a sword? Finally, I signed us up for a weekly program at the rectory:

Aesthetic Camp:
Tea and Shortbread and Intellectual Discussion
Of Topical Topics !
Saturday's Topic: Virginia Woolf on War!

The shortbread was really the big draw for us, but we soon discovered we were supposed to *bring* the shortbread ourselves — it was a brown bag sort of deal — and can't you just imagine how pissed Alan was when the shortbread didn't show? Can't you just picture the looks on the faces of the ladies from the Lovers of Lap Animals Club when Alan started yelling "Don't you stupid cat masturbators know who I am? I started the Bay City Rollers, goddammit — do you think I need your fuckin' shortbread?"

At least that's what I *thought* he said, but do I need to tell you that was the end of Aesthetic Camp?

Oh Marianne, where did it all go wrong? Was it the manager? The heroin? The brain damage? Do you think I should leave him? I'm only twenty years old — don't I deserve my piece of the American dream? Don't I deserve to have a job down at City Hall and order from Avon? To eat pizza in bed while watching "Star Wars" on tv?

Misty

The bar is on the outskirts of Kankakee County, and you are looking out a small window at an empty highway, bright with rain. The sizzling of the infrequent cars reminds you of the wet concrete windowsills of the Leland Hotel on Harrison, and that night last autumn with the civil servant from Sheboygan. The sensation of rain cuts through you, and your cold bones buzz. There is a smell of gin and unwashed hair. You sense that the smell was here before the bar, and once the bar was built the smell settled into the woodwork and decided to stay for life.

You look down and a young man and an older woman are sitting at a small table and she is lifting his chin with her index finger and he is looking away. She takes a cigarette out of a case and it reminds you of the chocolate cigarettes in the green plastic cases you used to get as a kid from Universal Candies on Ashland. You imagine her cigarettes smell like that — cold and clean.

At the pinball machine a dwarf in a striped shirt squirms, beating your high score.

At the bar a large woman encumbers a nervous man. She exudes a perfume —"If you like Charlie, try Fragrance 13" — in her straight oiled auburn hair and in the spaces between her fingers. She bought it in the Woolworth's on State Street when she went shopping with her girlfriend. The girlfriend went back to her job at the cashier's window in City Hall and she stayed to buy panties and a pair of red plastic shoes. The man is twitchy clean, too small in his ill-fitting suit with the big patch pockets, worried because her smell is adhering to the threads. He is nerve-wracked, thinking of his young daughter, alone at home for the first time.

The bartender spits on a wine glass, polishes it, then holds it up to the dim light for inspection. He grips the glass by the stem, fills it with white wine, and brings it over to your end of the bar, to the young girl sitting two stools down. She picks up the glass with her skinny hand and raises it to her mouth. Too much 69 cent Wet and Wild "Laser Pink" lipstick leaves a half ring on the rim. She sits between two men, burly blonds, looking up giggly at them, a little flirty, a little frightened. She's too drunk to remember where she met them: by the side of the cemetery? in front of the all-night currency exchange? behind the discount clothing store?

She slips her shoes on and off, the ones she bought on Milwaukee Avenue the day she had bad cramps, and the salesman at the counter made a pass at her, and she felt uncomfortable, braless in a skimpy spring car coat. Her feet are cold and pale and dry. Her ripped stockings were stolen from her mother. They smell like cigarettes and feet. She wears them to school sometimes, and the teachers know there is something about her: it is in the way she glances—a sort of straining of her heavily-lined eyes under the brows, under the cotton-candy hair. She is always late, her stale shirt always wrinkled, her gamey jeans worn and bent at the knees.

The two men look sidelong at her, and down. The first three buttons of her blouse are undone, but when she moves a certain way you can see that they're actually missing. She's telling them she doesn't like school, the homeroom nun smells of detergent and bleach, and the area right around her nails is always dry and white and flaking. The men look at her, and then at each other, then ask more questions until the time is right. She sees them looking at each other and she glances over at them and she looks at the bartender and then at you. You are about to say something to her, to disengage her from the men, but the large woman behind you suddenly laughs raucously and her gums become visible — blue-veiny, coated in white — and the dwarf beats his own high score, and the two men motion to the girl that it is time to leave, and she plucks herself up and they surround her, and it's too late to say anything. The bartender watches them from the far end of the bar.

Looking out the small window you watch them cross the bright empty highway in silence. It has stopped raining. The closing door ushers in the smell of attics and old things, the smell that lingers after a rain. The girl recalls that smell from some time ago: the smell of a kid named Kevin in the prairie behind the house. She used to play there, sometimes with the kids of her father's friends who came over to see the tvs and radios and record players her father fixed up and sold for cheap when he was out of work. One afternoon it was hot and her mother had slapped her for talking back, and she went to lie between the overgrown grasses of the prairie. She was eleven. She lay on her back, closed her eyes and since the sun was hot and high she could see purple and pink and white flowers inside her eyes. She heard the grass crashing and she turned her head. She heard a mouse die when Kevin stepped on it as he came closer and asked her what she was doing there like that. Was she waiting for something? He knelt down next to her, smelling of attics and old things and mossy clothes at the bottom of a closet, and said he wanted to show her something . . .

They pass a bus barn. The two men clasp the girl by the elbows, steering her. It is irritating but she doesn't mind, really — it reminds her of the way the cops always held her those times she got arrested. One bus is about to leave. Its headlights flare and she is blinded and everything is blue.

The bus driver sees the three forms ignited and haloed and he turns his transistor radio dial. "Misty" is playing. He likes hearing "Misty" now, while it's raining and he knows his wife is home alone sleeping, her soft body curled up in the bed. Sometimes in spring he fantasizes a woman will board his bus very late at night, a beautiful, furtive woman, pulling her shabby, second-hand raincoat around her body. She will lie down on the floor of the bus at his feet, and he will turn off the lights so that the bus looks abandoned to anyone who might be absently gazing through their fiberglass curtains on their way back from the bathroom. Then afterwards she will smooth out the wrinkles in her raincoat, pull it tightly around her, smile sadly and hop off.

But then the driver sees the man with a gun coming in through the door, and he scatters from his seat, which the man with the gun assumes. As the driver jumps off the bus his eyes meet the eyes of the girl. Her odd calmness, the cool in her eyes like that of cats, shocks the driver, and he goes running off, flailing in the gravel toward the public phone, a ghostly sentry at the far end of the depot.

The floor of the bus is annoying to the back of the girl's head. She can feel the butt ends of cigarettes, wet from soggy shoes, inside the little valley between her upper neck and skull. The floor smells of nicotine and spit. The man at the wheel is driving fast. He yells to a woman clutching a big purse and waiting scared at the stop, "Only good-lookin' chicks on this bus!" The man on top of the girl begins to work mechanically, like a crab, like a tool, moving her legs apart with his knee. His breath on her nose makes her close her eyes. She turns her head away so she can open her eyes and, straining, sees ball after ball of light —the streetlights, punching past. The rhythms hypnotize her, and she wonders if the two men are planning a robbery, or a murder, and whether they'll kill her, too. She figures they'll probably want to.

As If

assembled from an email: the "Worst Similes in High School Essays" competition

I'm still trying to forget everything that happened. But the memory of it sticks, like old gum to the bottom of a classroom chair, or a church pew when you reach underneath because you're bored at Sunday mass or something.

I looked out the window: it was raining, and hailstones were leaping on my windowsill like maggots when you fry them in hot grease. Across the meadow, on the pond, a little boat floated gently on the calm water, like a bowling ball wouldn't. Except for the rain, nothing was different about my typically suburban neighborhood: the white picket fences like Nancy Kerrigan's teeth, the red brick buildings the color of a brick-red Crayola crayon.

Suddenly from above me there came an unearthly scream. Suddenly there was an eerie surreal quality to everything — like when you're on vacation in another city and "Jeopardy" comes on at 7 instead of 7:30. My thoughts became all jumbled, like underwear in a dryer without Cling-Free. And then came the first crash of thunder, ominous-sounding, like the sound of a metal sheet being shaken backstage during a scene in a play. Then I saw it: a body falling from the apartment window above me, hitting the ground like a Hefty bag filled with soup. It had caught my eye like one of those pointy hook-latches that dangle from screen doors and fly up into your eye whenever you open the door.

I assumed the person was dead. But they got up, unharmed, as if they were Wile E. Coyote in a Road Runner cartoon. I could see they were a man, and he was tall like a tree, like a six-foot three-inch tree. His hair glistened in the rain like your upper lip when you have a runny nose, and his eyes were big, like two big brown circles with black dots in the centers. He started looking around for something, then he smiled and waved, as if he'd just arrived in town on a Greyhound bus and someone was rushing across a crowded street to meet him. Then I could see a woman, rushing across the meadow toward him, as if she were rushing across a crowded street to meet someone who'd just arrived in town on a Greyhound bus. Long separated by cruel fate, these star-crossed lovers began racing toward each other like two freight trains, one having left Cleveland at 6:36 pm, traveling at 55 mph, the other from Topeka at 4:19 pm, at a speed of 35 mph. I wondered if maybe they'd never even met before, like two hummingbirds who'd also never met before.

They finally embraced, and I could hear them talking. They were talking loud, shouting to be heard above the storm, like Helen Hunt and that other actor in the movie *Twister.* He shouted with a calm certainty that only comes with experience, like a guy who went blind because he looked at a solar eclipse without one of those boxes with a pinhole in it, and now goes around the country speaking at high schools about the dangers of looking at a solar eclipse without one of those boxes with a pinhole in it. Her vocabulary was as bad as...whatever. By that time I had to tear myself away from the window because I really had to go to the bathroom. And when I went it was like a great flood of yellow water breaking through a dam made of porcelain. When I got back to the window they were gone, unnoticed, like the period after the "Dr." on the Dr. Pepper can. I was disappointed, like someone reading a badly written story where the two main characters suddenly disappear for no good reason whatsoever, and that's the end of the story.

Eleusis

1.

My mother offers me tranquilizers like a kid sharing a stash of candy. I sit down on the cot opposite her bed and watch her undress. Like any Anglo-Saxon, I know nothing of the fungal world, but she defines for me the source of all unnatural splendor, half-exotic, half-dead.

"I never suffered anything in my life like the last six and a half hours," she says. "Hand me that Romilar. Listen, when we were kids we didn't have Romilar—we used the roots of a tree!"

She smells of tobacco, bed sweats, bloat. She spends half her time in that bed reading romance magazines, scandal sheets, eating, coughing, spitting up. Every moment with her is another nightmare. I've just come off a week of living in an utter void of sight and sound, crescendoing with my passing out naked in the Dog Hole, a South Side bar. Now here, in this badly paneled bedroom, the long dark night of the soul is occurring spontaneously every five minutes, and I'm beginning to wonder just how a human psyche can bear witness to this kind of crustacean horror, normally buried deep within it.

* * * * *

By noon she's throwing her voice directly into my psyche:

"I got palpitations of the brain pans, what they call it. It's my *harmones*! They keep gettin' more 'n' more delicate! Hyperstatic, how they call it. Listen, hand me a Tranxene. You need one? I got ten right here. First, put a tv dinner in."

Syllables flying off, frayed, hasty, in jerks. Talk, talk. Listen, listen. Each of my five senses a convenient conduit for her seemingly accidental tortures. The anguish of hearing thousands of ill-conjugated verbs. She exhibits that legendary tendency of the Nordic-Teutonic nature to discern the potential for torture in any situation. I have abandoned all belief in my revival. No one will find me here where invisibility is the same as failure. I wonder if anyone has noticed that I'm dead and if so whether they've taken the trouble to mourn me. Outside the streets are being cleaned, like on the weekend.

2.

I used to be a drunk, and that made me a citizen of the world. A cut-rate parasite, welcome anywhere. The 14th Ward regulars knew they could count on me for a few drinks, sometimes even a bottle of pills depending on who I'd slept with. Back then we were so familiar. Of course I was always impeccably groomed and ready to manipulate exquisite verbal resources, launching my listeners into diverse worlds of classrooms, country clubs, funny farms, public toilets. I was also blessed with a metropolitan fame based on a complete disregard for my personal safety. I could drop in anytime through the night entrance of the Dog Hole and immediately sink into a delicious lethargy, my chloroform bottle at the ready. On my last night of freedom I had made my way through the verminous shadows hunched over broken tables to the back room, where Pete, the alderman's assistant, held forth.

"Have you seen the latest acquisition?" he asked, then handed me a vial containing a mixture of barley ergot and mint—the legendary *kykeon.*

"Blissful is he," winked Pete, invoking the Eleusinian benediction, "who has been initiated into the Holy Mysteries, who knows the end of life as well as its beginning."

"Blissful is she," I answered, in accordance with the ancient and accepted rite, "who has received Reason and dies with Hope."

He mixed the kykeon in a silver goblet with the tibia of a pig and handed it to me. My first feeling was a bottomless terror. The fitful wind I'd been hearing became a vast wheel, constantly accelerating. Then the wheel became a gondola, sweeping majestically through moonlit lagoons, then an eagle careening me up, Alp over Alp, then down into the primeval forest where my soul metamorphosed into some kind of giant vegetable, an eggplant maybe. I continued as an eggplant for what felt like days even though it was only about three minutes tops. Then from the very bottom of my despair I heard a voice like a tremendous engine full of sublime cadences, the voice of a multitude of deaths. It began as a jet of pulsating air and nerve, then crackled into a nasal whine, softened by phlegm, tinged with banality and fear. From beneath the cathedral archway of giant fern I heard:

"What kinda dummy sits in a queer bar gettin' stupid drunk?"

It was her. Her voice. And she was bending over me, the warm hole of her mouth the center of all cigarette roses, disgorging with every word the legion demon agents of my transformation. How had I found my way back to her plastic-covered couch? That was just the beginning. The Word made fleshy.

3.

The afternoon ritual: a perversion of the very idea of repetition as comfort. She stretches out across the bed to make contact with a blue box of ice cream cones, her favorite snack. Everything about her is vivid colors: the Wonder Bread bag, the little boxes of sugary breakfast cereals, the cheap striped cotton tops, and when she goes to Lulu's, the red-orange trailer across the street where she buys her milk, bread, cigarettes and Lotto, she wears a green scarf over her thin, graying pin curls. All she has to do is move, or not move, and all the horrors and ignominies of a life spent with her begin flowing again, real fast, like an Ethiopian funeral mass.

"Y'know, I'm not like you," she says today and will surely say tomorrow, pulling a cone out of the box, "I don't need an audience. Now go get me a Kleenex."

* * * * *

Always at about seven o'clock we enter the second phase of everyday, like a lime-green Rambler jauntying towards inevitable disaster. The endlessly garish tv shows, the families in their big sweaters in their comfortable homes, the women well-fed, their cherry lips perfect. From the plastic-covered couch I watch the cars go by outside and begin again my fantasy of the perfect all-night diner, its fake ferns, ceiling lights and fans a beacon in the feathery night, proclaiming the comfort of whatever I want, they got.

* * * * *

Midnight begins with her hot breath filling the bedroom — *I got th' devil lookin' over my shoulder . . . Aw now where th' hell are them Tranxenes?* — and the sickly tv sheen moving mauve-to-violet-to-green in the living room where I lie on the couch, watching the shadows stirring as they seek form. The heady nausea accompanying the rapid succession of ideas that replaces sleep can be categorized in three ways: what I'm thinking/what I need now/who I should have been by now. And the reality: I wanted to be an angel; I have become a beast. Everything implied by the word "chance" has turned on me to reveal the depth of my mediocrity; I am, in fact, a kind of patron saint of mediocrity, a Saint Teresa of Avila pierced by the arrow of all that has been and will forevermore be Lost.

I recall the good old days when by merely going to dinner I could scandalize everyone. The good old days of "I can't run in these earrings!" Now, enthralled by oppressive thoughts that come sudden, perfect and inevitable, I can comfortably anticipate extraordinary pain the like of which the man in the street will never know. This certainty becomes the very archetype of my psyche's precise annihilation. I am a being truly transformed by the purity of complete mediocrity.

Later, just before dawn I hear, from somewhere near my ear: *The god of sleep is the same as the god of healing.*

Later. Within the safety of an endless stream of thoughts

the night progresses to its end mysteriously, piously, like the Canticle of the Ancient of Days.

4.

Dawn's milky light reveals only enlarged pores and the results of a recent $7 haircut. The light overflows its shafts that stripe the bathroom tiles and fuses into a single intense instantaneous feeling of eternity. Who was I before this light and what did I do and what did I think?

I suppose she's still asleep. But soon she will grow, swell and burst like a meteor—coughing, shuffling, smoking and flailing into the bathroom then back to the bed, and this halo of nostalgia for the present will disappear forever like prehistory's first lost tribe.

I go into her room, as I do every morning, to see if she's still breathing. I listen for the little "putts" of breath coming from behind her skinny lips. But today there are no little "putts." She's dead. I sit down on the cot across from her bed. I look at her hard round head, her mouth open as if she were trying to form the perfect vowel.

I sit on the cot across from her bed and watch the hours swing down to afternoon. I wonder how long I can sit here with her body. I like having her body in this room. No one in the neighborhood knows; they are all going about their business and we are alone, just the two of us, and the memories her body has released to me. She is my new all-night diner, her body a beacon of comfort in the feathery dark. She for whom I sacrificed everything. Now I have nothing. No thing. Tonight we will both be able to sleep.

5.

It's the warm yellow morning of a busy day. The languid and astonished condition of giddiness replaces any memory of past unhappiness. Outside I can hear the neck bells of invisible horses. I think of the punishments I've suffered and the comfort of this new insatiable thirst for clarity. Thus I see no great danger in breaking free, despite the certainty of losing a bit of dignity: I can call any 7-11 in the country and be assured they're serving strong, shiny coffee.

What I know now: Reality is the raw material for the process of personal demise as The Great Work. My ego feeds exclusively now on the certainty of my immediate and eternal ruin. Like Chiron I have been mortally wounded, but through my sacrifice at the hard red hands of the Mother I am immortal and cannot die. This is my punishment. But like the hanged man, whose orgasm is not a gesture of submission but a gift from the Tree of the Knowledge of Good and Evil, I have received nothing less than ultimate Reason here, and can live on forever in purest Joy. The lost are lost by destiny, and destiny starts early and falls naturally one thing to the next like an old man's lazy game of dominoes on the summer stoop.

I speak to you now in her own flat, spent idiom: on the day you wake beyond the Pleiades, remember me to the One who lived here:

she once was a true love of mine.

Experiment

During the writing of my last novel I found myself stricken with writer's block. I decided to shake things up by sleeping with the first man I encountered in the next store I went into, which turned out to be the HMV on 34th and 6th.

That man, a clerk in the sound track section, looked like the roly-poly guy who plays Newman on *Seinfeld*. Roly-poly isn't my type, but I had to stick to my guns.

"Let's fuck," I said, taking him by surprise.

"Right here," I said, pointing to the floor. "Take your clothes off."

The faux-Newman's girth turned out to be a problem: how to fit both of us in the space between the checkout counter and the wire basket full of blank cassettes? Somehow we managed. Shoppers crowded around: some excited, some deeply offended. A beefy security guard ran over and threatened us by brandishing his walkie-talkie in our faces.

"Listen," I said, "don't come in me. I'm not on the Pill."

Faux-Newman pulled out, and I was alarmed to see drops of dark orange pee shooting from his penis, mixed in with the stream of dishwatery come. I wondered if I'd get some kind of infection. I wondered where my underwear was.

Just then a woman loomed above us, remonstrating with my partner. Turned out it was his mother. We both scrambled to our feet and dressed quickly. I still couldn't locate my underwear so I got dressed without it.

The woman corralled us into the break room and gave us what for. Turned out faux-Newman *was* the guy who played Newman on *Seinfeld*. He was preparing for his starring role in a new sitcom about a hapless clerk in the sound track section of HMV. And the woman, his mother, would be playing opposite him on the show as the slave driver owner of all HMVs. I asked if there might be a part for me on the show.

"The only thing you need to worry about, little missy," she said, "is where your underwear is."

Luck

I'd say my most harrowing life experience was that time I lost Mayor Koch at the airport. It was during my marriage to Jerry, and Jerry and the Mayor were like this, which was how I got the job as His Honor's Personal Travel Trainer in the first place. I worked right under Bess Myerson — so to speak.

Jerry was making a picture called *King of Comedy* and this was my first big job in the world. I had to make sure the Mayor got up extra early on the days he was traveling, did his usual calisthenics plus the special hydro-propelled pelvic thrusts, ate his special breakfast, and went to the bathroom without straining. (We always referred to it as "getting lucky " But that's between you and me.)

On this particular day His Honor was coming back from a promotional tour of the Rose Bowl floats being made out in Pasadena, and I was there at the airport to greet him with a papaya baked to be slightly leathery on the outside, just in case he hadn't been "lucky" that morning. My two gals and I were told to wait in a separate terminal area for the Mayor because the heat in the usual terminal was off. So we waited and waited for an hour, but no Mayor Koch. On top of that, only one of the Mayor's bags had arrived, and the backpack where he carried all his "Seek-a-Word" puzzles was still a no-show. I kicked up a fuss with one of the airport lackeys, a stiff named Dandles, and finally finagled my way onto the loudspeaker system. I paged His Honor myself and told him to meet us by the taxi stand. Sure enough, we found him there, madder than a monkey with a wet banana. He didn't even want his papaya. Well too bad, I thought, and forced it on him, then sent him off to the toilet and had it cordoned off for two hours — there was no way I was going to deal with a backed-up Edward I. Koch. Meantime, one of my gals had called Jerry and he showed up to lend moral support.

"Listen kid," he said, putting his arm around me, "after

Ed poops the world's a different place. You know I wrote a song about that once? Slim Whitman recorded it. I don't make a big deal about it or anything. But now we got two hours — let's go to the movies."

I never knew that some airports had movie theatres! But Jerry knew — he broke ground for the first one back in 1952 with Dean. So we settled in with a bunch of tipsy stewardesses to watch *Pal Joey* while Ed got busy getting lucky.

But I couldn't sit still. I was worried about the goddamn bags. So I slipped out and tried to navigate back to the main terminal. I felt like I was in *Twilight Zone* — all those endless anonymous corridors leading to more endless anonymous corridors, and then my worst fear times two: a mouse and a rat. They attached themselves to the bottom of my peasant skirt and wouldn't let go! I was running and screaming and screaming and running, but luckily my hysteria propelled me right back to the main terminal and the bright lights scared the little creeps off me. And there was His Honor! Sitting on a broken baggage carousel like he was Mr. Anybody, American.

"No luck, kid," he said sadly.

"I'm sorry," I said, putting my arm around him. "And no bags, either. But Jerry's here. Wanna go to the movies?"

My Life in Yonago

Grief
After mass, became drunk, fell down, and made violent love to nobody.

Sunstroke
Luncheon at the Pox Hospital with Mother. Enjoyed a billowy seaside melancholy, like one who was born bourgeois.

Asthma
At the Stag County Kosher Smorgasbord, Mother and I dined with the Japanesians on a delicacy that translates as "ass bacon." The rabbi offered to sterilize any objects on our persons, "even a straight pin." After a brief stop at the Acme Sitting Station, we visited the Pit of Thespians.

Vicious Vices of Early Life
Money is round, and runs away; love finds us young, and ruins the purse.

Parents Were Cousins
Father was an intense and revolutionary simpleton, tetched in the head. He blossomed as a poet during the heyday of Public Bath #7, his verse a flare-up of early corn-fed communism. After years of living in the cheap hotels of world bohemias he became chronically ill with painter's colic, unrelieved by gravel-weed, and retired to Graz, where he met Mother, she of the bluest of Austrian bloodlines. She appeared one day in the office of Dr. Pellagrio Robinson, inventor of remedies for syphilis and scrofula, and she seemed to Father to be the perfect expression of that nostalgic post-war Rhineland-based dadaism, that blatantly subtle *krankenkunst*. Her first words to Father, as she lay spread-eagled in Robinson's stirrups, were: "It is incumbent upon us *übermenschen* to be insane for awhile, like the steam in the nozzle of a tea kettle." That night Father escorted her to

a costume ball at the Dill Pickle. She came naked, head shaved, loins girded by kittles. William Carlos Williams admired her postage stamp beauty. After marriage and cuckolding they returned for a time to the Rhineland, and founded a steam room. Then came Mother's McKinley Jefferson.

Political Excitement

I am a genius, and my famous liver is more than wondrous. I claim spawnage from water, flour, and awkwardness. My mental equipment is ephemeral and splenetic, and I will reveal more liver later. I will be tender, yet contemptuous.

Religious Excitement

My mustache smelled like a party as Mother and I departed on the Australian tramp steamer *Teheran*. We were planning to demonstrate to the idolaters of Ceylon the necessity of adopting our practice of ascetic rectal contentment. Parting with sincere regret from the Admiral and Mrs. Niven Scrims, we were soon augmented by Cornelius Blauveldt and Mrs. Blitzer, a dowager easily frightened by cars. During our passage we sang the beloved hymn that begins, "Inlaid with brightest gold .... " (Hyperbole, of course, to any Australian.) Our first impression of Ceylon was that a Dutchman in any branch of the coconut business would surely thrive there, for Ceylon's imports are its exports and vice-versa. (The business of cinnamon, however, is strictly controlled by Jews.) It seemed that the Ceylonese might do well to return to a state of amphibiousness, or at least luxuriant vegetation: the women are denied a crowning ornament, and the men are naked save for a kittle. According to Mrs. Blitzer, both sexes are phallists, and thus it is that any minister who dares teach these heathens is regarded as a prodigy. Blauveldt stated that the deepest longing of the Ceylonese heart is for the correct aesthetic display of indoor fruit. Murmurers at the frontier, said Mother, spoke of a colonial history marked by years of mattresses supplied by the grim priests of St. Fig. Our mission was to investigate recent disruptions in the Law of Inherited Tendencies, and whether pearls are indeed formed by swallowing babies.

Overaction of the Mind
After mass, Mother becomes expansive and demanding — a fascinating study of our slippery relation to reality.

Women
Two tiny sisters from Holland.

Business Nerves
The bad air was vitiated by breathing. There were gases and all sorts of foul matters held in suspension. From the putrid soil hair particles, decomposing vegetable and animal products, stray cotton fibers, and bits of artificially insulated wires sprang in abundance. The vegetable kingdom contributed seeds, spores, buds, bobs, pods, pollens, pistils, and light floating bodies. From the animal world were conducted bits of tissue. Tooth holes produced molds. The secretions of publicly promiscuous individuals caused croup. If any person had taken the trouble to stand in the sun and look at his own shadow on a plastered wall, he would've easily perceived his body to be a festering mess of corruption, exuding subtle, acrid smoke that caused thick frogs to fibrillate. Sitz baths, the buttermilk purge, and a general cultivation of mirth were employed, all to nil effect. In a last-ditch effort, statues were savaged for cold metal poultices.

Intemperance
My collection of Amish wiggle pictures: meticulously pilfered from Aggie Svoboda.

Jealousy
The arm of Aggie Svoboda
Braldt Braldts and his *Dun'no Eulogy*
Cousin Edna (and Snooky)
Buster Charneck: dervish at the bat
Mother's McKinley Jefferson
Herb

Kicked in the Head by Horse
I was born in 1895 in Orzo, and made my living as a grower. My early problems with discharges were remedied by an elasticized truss-girdle. Around 1903 I invented a machine to vitiate sitz baths by means of a gummy rectal tube, but my idea was stolen by Herb, who profited from it and fled. This contributed to the relapse of discharge. With Mother's help I began my current work of perfecting a whirling machine — half loom, half balloon — for deducing futility.

Bite of Rattlesnake
The shameful bird's nest antidote.

Fever and Loss of Lawsuit
One day it came to my attention that religion and wisdom were possible only to the lowly-minded. Thus I began to live my life in accordance with the maxim, "The Greatest Gifts of Mother Nature are Packed in a Manly Bosom." For a week I embarked upon preaching. Soon after, however, I learned firsthand the misery of "the monsignor's complaint."

Bad Company
After mass, Herb began to exhibit an assaultive, Old World arrogance.

Bad Habits
Herb abjured me to ask, "Mother, do you have something in your purse for the duck?"

Doubt About Mother's Ancestors
Just as Alexander the Great learned drunkenness from a manservant and cruelty from a barber, Mother learned magnetism from a banister. She dazzled her own generation, but merely wearies ours.

Seduction and Disappointment

Herb's sudden injunction struck a cold chord with my virtue, but my fallow mind produced few misgivings. My coat was rent as if without seams ("Kingly robes," he taunted, "cause wakeful nights.") And so it is: nobility lives free of fear, and the heart uses friendship for food. In good time, the savage bull began battering the yoke. Like a brazen Bavarian I bewitched him, and soon his snout took to rooting. Thus inspired, I bared my rutter. The exhibition made him vicious: he tore the tops of my cottons with his teeth, forged a gorge upon my pate, then insisted upon shifting to the trundle. I volleyed; he parried: "Birds with bright plumage do not make good pie"! The subtle knave was expunged, and I discharged a fog forthwith. Oh, but what becomes of honor once exposed to obloquy! Its final cry like that of a tiny kitten driving an ambulance.

Carbuncle

These occur when vitality is inactive, or in disrepair. If the mass of flesh is ripe and come to a head, it should be cut freely and deeply, the core sucked or scraped, and the thick gluten allowed to flow. Often the fault lies with the heart, or some other organ.

Acid Gas

The lowly pineapple is a complete medicine cabinet in itself.

Indigestion

Another result of calumny. Cured by ingesting the tannins of pine boughs, scooped from the Sheholy, where the *schaum* coagulates.

Cold

A direct result of my calumny, but cured with coal oil and turpentine. Black pepper and desiccated egg were applied to the spine, as recommended by Robinson, and bandages of camphor, per the Japanesians.

Softening of the Brain

Mother had me run to the junction for her *Women's Comfort* publication (which used to be sold only on subscription by the Blue Roses Ladies). Shiftless men lolled about around Buster Charneck's kiosk. I put it straight to them: What is illicit in the morning, eclectic in the afternoon, and pretentious yet uncivilized at night? Accustomed as they were to violent exercising and straining at stool, they were not fit to answer. Their antipathy rushed over me like a fetid fantailing sea, and they removed me to the fruitcage. Only days later was I extricated, owing to the obscene gestures of Mother's McKinley Jefferson.

Gathering in the Head

Accompanied Cousin Edna and girlfriend Ova to the annual festival of St. Roustino. Amidst boisterous *semina* sellers and deliciously exposed *mameaux* we shouldered our way to the front of the fray, for the passing of the car, pulled by a tractor, as the search for an ox had been in vain. This year the car was a huge, cathedral-shaped affair of intricately carved white marzipan cornices, balustrades, parapets, and tabernacles. Around the stern knelt naked Brownies in attitudes of angst, and beneath them, along the prow, the tiered sections for the quintet jutted out. Above all towered Roustino, the Hanged Angel, in effigy. The suffocating crowd pushed, shoved and elbowed, and quite often I caught a *mameau* in the mouth. Scores fainted. An entire balcony collapsed, and those who fell upon spectators were murdered. Braldt Braldts, assuming the proscenium, intoned his *Dun'no Eulogy,* and then, as if the sky had fallen, the shouts of stampeders grew deafening as Snooky appeared as "Dulcie," straddling the pinnacle. She was taken to task by stevedores, who arranged her in the usual posture: hips aloft, she expelled the blessing. Oilcloths were spread to protect spectators from effluvia. Buster Charneck, overwhelmed by confusion, had to be removed.

Imaginary Female Troubles
Inability to carry crockery, instability of the voluntary muscles, deranged uterine functions, quinsy of the mucous-membranes, noise and hoarseness, summer diarrhea, sore nipples, involuntary lactation, phlegmasia dolens ("milk-leg"), sexual organs unresponsive to vigorous manipulation, sexual organs blistered or missing, sick headache and nervous sick headache, great varieties of discharge, involuntary shedding of tears, playfulness, sleeping outdoors, watching, flannel-craving, repetitive stretching and yawning, repression of urine, constant spitting, onset of menses, falling bowel, chills in the teeth, relaxation of the vessels of the true skin with simultaneous elevation of the scarf-skin, sensation of ice melting in the stomach, fistulas in the vicinity of the anus, and strainings exacerbated by the irrigations of worms.

Snuff Eating for Two Years
After his war wound resumed, Herb habitually compelled me to strip and wear earrings, massive pendulous earrings, and alternately crawl, run, and mimic swimming while he photographed me from behind. But I just couldn't run in those earrings.

Laziness
After some muscular conjuring with Mother, we leave Yonago.

Harm

My walking tour of the southern states got messed up
after Texas. I stayed too long in Amarillo with a trucker and
got a ride to the border. I waited for an hour and another
trucker came along. The next thing I knew I was sitting on
a lawn in a hick town somewhere. Everyone who walked
by was drunk, or off somehow. Even their shadows were
off. One guy walked up to me and said, "You sleep with niggers, don't you?"

I had to get somewhere safe. A woman went by with a
package. She had stringy hair and a bad complexion. She
looked like she was going home, so I approached her.

"Excuse me," I said, "I don't mean to bother you but I
need help. I'm not sure where I am and I just need to get a
glass of water. Can I step into your place momentarily? I
won't stay long."

"Sure," she said, "come right in. I was just about to put
supper on. And listen — if my husband's drunk, don't mind
him, okay? He don't mean no harm."

We walked into a narrow kitchen. It smelled like old
fried chicken. The living room was just big enough for a
couch and a chair. It was lit by a bare lightbulb hanging
from the ceiling. The breeze from the door made it swing
and cast jerky shadows. A bony man was sprawled on the
couch with a bottle in his lap. A little girl with matted black
hair was playing with eggs on the floor, balancing them on
their sides. The man watched indifferently. When I came in
he waved weakly.

"Come right in," he said. "We're the Andersons. Just sit
down there on the floor. We ain't got no more chairs."

The little girl perked up and said, "See? See what I'm
doing?"

I knelt down near her. I didn't want to disturb the eggs.
She seemed different from everything around her: bright
and alert, not the product of those two at all. She had black
hair and they were both blondes. Just then a lion appeared

at the back window.

"Is there a zoo around here?" I asked.

"Nah," said the man. "There's a guy down the street owns him. Lets him out at night. Don't worry — the lion don't mean no harm."

The lion came in through a big hole in the screen door. It nuzzled up to me, pressing itself against my chest. Its big paws upset the eggs. The little girl didn't seem worried. We both stroked its mane.

Then the man pulled a gun out from the couch cushions. The woman backed off into the kitchen. He went in there, too. The little girl hugged the lion and squeezed her eyes shut. I heard a sound like steel drawers being opened and shut. When I peeked into the kitchen the man had tied the woman up with rubber tubing. She was sitting in the sink. Then he shot her.

I grabbed the little girl and we ran through the big hole in the screen to look for a policeman. There was a ball field in the distance, and I could make out two cops busting somebody. I shouted "Police! Police!" They didn't even look up.

"A guy just shot his wife!" I shouted. "This is their daughter!"

"Yeah, so what?" one of them answered. "Somebody's always shootin' their wife."

"Wait! I'll help," said a voice from the squad car. It was a lady cop dressed as a prostitute. We got in the car and she drove us back to the house. When we got there the lion had been shot, too. I was sadder about the lion than I was about the lady. The lion was noble and kind. The little girl would be homeless now. The man was back sitting on the couch, like nothing had happened.

"You gonna arrest me, lady? I don't think so. No lady can arrest me."

But the lady cop was tough. She arrested him. He took her seriously then. We all rode in her squad car to the station. No one talked. The little girl looked out the window and sang "Jumpin' Jack Flash" quietly to herself:

"Gas, gas, gas."

The station was dreary, like the house and everything else in the town. The lady cop steered Mr. Anderson into a room for questioning. The little girl and I followed. When Anderson took his hand out of his pocket I saw that he had a miniature gun duct-taped to his palm. I quickly left the room and told another cop to come in and help. He came in and quickly put his own gun over Anderson's gun. The lady cop winked at me.

"Good work!" she said. I felt terrific.

But there was the problem of the little girl. Where would she go? Where would I go? My clothes were torn and the tops of my shoes were cut off. It was hard to walk. The lady cop said she would drive us to the train station. I said I needed to buy some clothes and shoes first.

"You're about the same size as me," she said. "How 'bout I loan you some clothes and you mail them back to me when you get to your next town?"

"Thanks," I said.

"You're taking the little girl, aren't you?" the lady cop said. I said I would. It would only be for a while. I'd work hard to find a family for her. I could finish my walking tour another time. I imagined the little girl with her new parents: a young couple laughing with her on the top of a grassy hill behind their suburban ranch house.

Storm

Ayumi told me not to expect much from Uedo, the oldest part of Tokyo, the part even the Japanese wanted to forget about. As we walked clutching our souvenir clay *kitsune* she explained how once a year a six-block stretch of Mejiro-dori was dug out, filled with water, and stocked with dolphins, in remembrance of an old Shinto fertility festival that might never have happened in the first place. Attendance dropped every year, she said, and the performers stank, but as a foreigner in search of adventure I was still curious.

Mejiro-dori's wooden bridges were draped with tattered flags. Plastic Astro Boys and Sailor Moons stood at either end. Already there was quite a crowd. A model of the ancient *Bidu Gakku*, with real beer flowing from the cornices, provided a nice welcoming arch. Everyone promenaded in wooden clogs. There was a general air of congeniality. It was hard to see the dolphins with the big crowd gathered on the curbs, but Ayumi led me up a stairway to a platform once used by dignitaries that afforded a better view.

"Why don't you swim with them?" she suggested. "It's a great favorite among the children."

After a moment's hesitation I decided to take her suggestion. I located a landmark — the ornate gates of the *tengu* tower — positioned myself to face it, slid back down along the banister, and burst through the crowd at the landmark, landing with a great splash in the water. A pair of dolphins approached me, but after the newness of me wore off they veered toward some kids. Disappointed, I thought of asking for my money back but then remembered the events were free. Emerging from the water, I was a source of amusement for the older people.

Separated from Ayumi I wandered about, hoping the noontime sun would dry my clothes. I discovered an advertisement for "performing ape men" at the next intersection. I was expecting to see hirsute men, but it was just guys in rubber ape masks with ape hair pasted onto their jeans. They were demonstrating difficult feats of gymnastics, but even that was no good. One of them was having some sort of episode. Instead of launching himself into the air he just kept huffing and puffing, working up steam for a cartwheel that never materialized. When he noticed me in my wet clothes he made obscene gestures which, in the Japanese culture, indicated that we'd been familiar as children. The crowd was pleased and amused and applauded his efforts, but I'd had enough.

Crossing onto wide Omotesando Boulevard I entertained an image of relaxing with a glass of iced green tea in Ayumi's lovely *tatami* house. How long would it take to walk there from here, I wondered? The streets were packed — Japanese teenagers dressed in Fifties greaser clothes did the twist, and young girls got up like the first flight attendants were giving out Hello Kitty tea whisks in front of Mister Donut. The pedestrian bridge was noisy with festival-goers giggling and scurrying in their summer kimonos — it had started to rain. I had little hope now of finding a cab, but miraculously one was idling beneath the bridge. The driver waved me in when he saw me. He already had someone in the front, which I happily discovered was Ayumi. Apparently she'd had the same escape in mind.

"Had enough festival?" she asked me, and we laughed.

"Yoyogi-koen," I told the driver. He didn't understand my pronunciation, so Ayumi repeated it. It was a relief to have Ayumi there. I hugged her from behind, hoping that doing so wasn't too forward.

Soon the rain began to come down hard. The sky turned greenish-grey. I wondered if we were in for a typhoon. The moment before a typhoon seemed so magical. The Japanese were accustomed to it, and so took a laissez-faire attitude. But I loved sitting on Ayumi's couch and watching the sky grow dark over Tokyo, drinking iced green tea and listening to "Layla" by Derek and the Dominoes.

Then we were in another part of town, which looked like Hong Kong in *The World of Susie Wong*, or Shanghai before the war: wooden houses on stilts, zinc roofs glowing against the dark sky, and canals filled with long boats resembling sampans. The gray water churned and crested; a strong wind was beginning. A large family rowed by in a long wooden boat, and waved at us. They wore mushroom-shaped hats. I thought for sure I'd finally found the lost Japan I'd been searching for, that mysterious place "Yonago" mentioned in the first American accounts. But then I saw it, to the right, in the distance — a whirling column.

"Tornado!" I said, grabbing Ayumi by her collar and pointing at it.

"Tornado?" she repeated.

The funnel was kicking up dust in the distance, moving quickly toward us. Traffic completely stopped and there was a general panic. Our driver was getting nervous. He'd been drinking vodka from a bottle hidden under the steering column, and now he was drinking even more. When I looked out the other window a second funnel was taking shape in the opposite direction. At its base was smoke and fire — everything it touched was catching on fire.

"What is it? What do you call it?" Ayumi asked. I realized this was the first tornado to ever hit Japan.

"Tornado!" I repeated.

"Tornado," she whispered.

The wind picked up, making a frightening noise. The rain turned to hail. Children and pets were tossed about, then lost forever. I cracked my window a bit to relieve the air pressure — something I remembered from growing up in the storm belt of the Plains. Hail came pelting against our skin and Ayumi shrieked in pain.

"Don't worry!" I yelled. "I know what I'm doing!"

The driver, infected with the general panic, threw open his door and fled screaming, bouncing wildly off the other cars. I had to bring him back.

"No!" Ayumi called. "Let him go!"

I couldn't. If I died the Japanese would forever regard me as a heroine. As it turned out the driver was so terrified, as well as drunk, it was easy to pull him off the windshield of an abandoned Volvo. I dragged him back into the cab and yelled at him to head for the shoulder. He seemed to understand, and drove into a construction path, over boulders and cement blocks. It was tricky going. We were all soaking wet and shivering.

Soon he found an exit and pulled off onto a side street which led us to a completely different part of town. The tornado hadn't even touched this neighborhood, which was fashioned to resemble a classic small American town: a white church gleamed in the sun, the barbershop had a real barber pole out front, there was a general store, and a park with a carousel and band shell. People strolled by in period clothes, but I couldn't put my finger on what period. The sky was blue, the grass was green. We were entranced.

Chiseled in the facade of a building with Doric columns was "Bank of Yonago."

"It's like the U.S., isn't it?" Ayumi laughed.

"Yes," I whispered, my eyes filling with tears. "It's Yonago."

The driver was crying, too. Above us, a rainbow shimmered on the crystalline air.

The Hours of a
Transfigured Night

To Rita

Sext — noon to 3pm: receptivity
None — 3pm to sunset: preparation
Vespers — sunset to 9pm: the calling
Compline — 9pm to midnight: awakening
Matins — midnight to sunrise: enlightenment
Lauds — sunrise to 6am: mystical union
Prime — 6am to 9am: reconciliation
Terce — 9am to noon: sanctification

Sext This is about an accident of memory, about degrees
and digressions, about memory and its lattice of troubles.
As you know, my life has been full of accidents. I must've
been born in an accident. This story began when I made
three wishes, when I prayed for mental suffering, physical
sickness, and a revelation of divine love. But, after all, I am
a nun, and nuns always pray for ridiculous things.

To affect the fulfillment of those wishes I had decided to
place myself in the presence of divine love by meditating
continually, receptive to everything, restricting my eating so
that my body would become an empty vessel, ready for filling. And I used the flying feeling that hunger imparts to
help imagine myself moving swiftly toward something, flying high above my appetite. The nuns moving in twos
toward the chapel at Sext blurred to one body, one overwhelming rush, and a few times I almost collapsed. But I
knew prudence and conventional thinking had to be sent
away for my mind to move beyond mundane moorings.

But for a time only quietude ensued, and days passed like
serene frescoes.

None Do you remember how easily I withdrew from the

world when I was fourteen, after my stepfather died? I was always anxious for exit, always alone in a room twisting my hands, feeling deep in my bones the shifting meanings of Time's stately progression. A gypsy friend of my mother's once told me that the planets aligned at my birth were arranged in inharmonious oppositions of inharmonious conjunctions, heightened by Plutonic trines and sextiles: love in the house of learning, messages in the house of secrets. A true child of Time.

I never knew my real father, and my mother left us shortly before her second husband, my stepfather, died. She was an Andalusian Gypsy by way of Mexico. My memories of her are framed by the smell of cheap perfume and cooking grease. She occupied a world fraught with innuendo and suggestion, vicious machinations and outright lies, where the enemy was always just beyond her vengeance, hiding and seeking, utilizing seemingly endless snares. No one could be trusted — especially one's family. She met my father while working as a 'waitress' in a Tijuana underworld club. There were dolls on the tables, and if the man found his waitress pleasing he'd take the doll upstairs to the whorehouse, and the madam would set him up with that particular girl. My mother managed to sneak her doll out of the club when she snuck out herself, to marry my father, and I myself took possession of the doll as she made ready to leave me. Before entering the convent I placed my mother's doll — naked, dirt-dark, agate-eyed, nipples painted pink — in the last pew of the local church, hoping some child would find her and take her home, maybe even grow to love her.

I remember the time my mother and I bathed together when I was a child, during the happy time before she met my stepfather. She held me against her wet breast in the meek light of morning, the frosted window concealing us from the boys and men playing catch in the yard. There was blood in the tub — she was having her period: washing me in her wine-dark sea, nourishing me with her soup of roots.

44

Vespers A little after sunset the vision I wished for finally began, and its sudden movement was like a great flood carrying me into a remote, innermost room. The first image was not what I'd expected: "You ugly monkey," I hear my mother hissing, her eyes wet and her big face coming toward me in the dark. "How could something like you come outta me? You musta got mashed up in there. I shoulda gotten ridda you before it was too late. Now it's too late. Too goddamn late." She's struggling to tie me to a chair, seal my mouth with tape, and shut me up in the closet. After the door slams I can hear her talking to herself, can smell her l'Aimant perfume, can hear the dull thud of her head hitting the wall when my stepfather shoves her around because he's mad that she's still not ready because she can't keep her brat under control. I'm five years old. It's New Year's Eve.

And then when it was almost night another image came: a torso, soft, un-muscled, smelling of soap — my stepfather in summer, his flaccid back preceding me down a hallway toward darkness, his long soggy socks. I hadn't thought, spoken, or written of him in years, believing that to do so would bring his memory on harder, like a seizure. I began to remember clearly how much I hated him, with a child's hatred that eventually is buried but never dies. He sucked the light out of my mother's life, saying it was for her own good, dragging her with him wherever he roamed. And while they ranged freely in the world I sat tied to a chair in the closet, blindfolded, mouth taped, my natural impulses imploded, but my head full of words and stories of motion and stillness, webs and nets.

Compline Then fear was awakened as my soul moved out onto a starless perimeter to receive a third image: my child face on a doll's naked, dirt-dark body, legs spread in front of a camera. And the feeling that things were flying by just outside the windows, and I was the still center of the vivid existence I coveted. I wanted the image to stop, but I knew that to purge the vision meant killing myself — like burning one's house to prevent the enemy from entering. But I held to my belief that I would be purified, that this was what I'd asked for: the mental sickness from which revelation comes. Like a painful ritual to restore innocence, I told myself at midnight. I would look fearlessly at everything.

Matins At last I remembered: It's raining and I'm walking behind his flaccid back down a hallway into a dark room where his hands pull images from a bath of water. Fruits and flowers. Webs and nets. Soft triangles of flesh. Each image pinned and glinting high above me. Then his smile, his smell of soap and cigarettes, his glossy paunch rolling over my knees, long soggy fingers, skinny lips, thick tongue. The bitterness of the water that leaks from him. That sticks to my lips like honey. The feeling of Time passing, leaving us behind. The feeling that he is on the forward edge of something continually moving in and gaining ingress, then pulling away, just at the moment when I am able to take in all of him.

Lauds Another memory: He's leaning against the hot surface of my face, taped and tied, licking it like a dog. He moves like a tool, turning on the little yellow kitchen lamp, lifting me onto the table, separating my legs, leaning in, releasing a beam of cigarette breath, showing me his tongue, telling me of its insistence, coaxing me open, wider. Like a dog. Like a tool.

Those boy rhythms of his coming in. Now I'm observing a night room from somewhere near the ceiling: he enters from the bathroom with a hot water bottle, a hose attached, holding it like some ancient Egyptian jar-bearer. I'm looking at myself on the floor, black plastic garbage bags, canned goods, and old clothes scattered around, and he's putting a pillow down, turning me around, turning my face sideways, placing a rubber ball in my mouth, I can taste it, raising my back onto a strap attached to a pulley, positioning me, inserting the hose. And then an excruciating pain, an overwhelming sickness, as the water flows into me, but I go through the pain like he taught me, roaming inside it until I see myself dilated like an eye, opened up wide, preparing a place for him, for the ocean of honey that is his gift, but feels like knives. Down under those boy rhythms. Down under the narrow-hipped boy. Knees as souvenirs. He turns me around and enters my mouth, taking a picture. *Me — the centerfold. And he is the interloper, an antelope.* Later, a photo framed in roses.

And now I'm remembering again, seeing this from inside this time, from my own point of view. It's 3 am and he's driving me home from somewhere. There are no cars, it's an unincorporated area, we pull into an empty warehouse parking lot and he tells me to take off my clothes. I'm nine years old. He ties a rope around me and pretends to ride me to the middle of the lot, my chest silty with stones. We stop under a spotlight and he enters me, striking me with the rope. When he reaches his climax he bellows — no one can hear him. Except me, from deep inside the pain again, as we rise like Venus the Evening Star and Lucifer the Bringer of Light, in grand transit across the night into morning. When we arrive home my mother has found the photographs. She has arranged them in a line across the kitchen table like a solitaire game. She gathers her bags up and leaves. Without me.

Prime You will not be shocked by what I'm now relating. And I accept this as the vision which comes from you. When I was fourteen I killed him.

It was a Saturday morning, early, maybe seven. I was sleeping and he came into my room, slipping under the covers, easing his hands under me, preparing to enter me. I want to try something new, I said. Something I've been planning. I told him to lay down under me, and he said, You know I don't like it this way. I promise, I said. And he did it, reluctantly. I went through all the motions, dipping into a repertoire of feminine gestures, and finally he moved in rhythm, and I felt like a boat on an undulant sea. I rode him harder. Harder still. Until his heart began to burst and he asked me to stop. But I kept on until I knew, and then went into the bathroom as it progressed, turning on the shower. When I came out he was gone, and I called the ambulance. Later I took a bus downtown, just to walk around: the heady feeling of being small beneath big buildings, of an insufficient blouse on a cool spring morning.

Terce Morning's glossy kiss. Across the courtyard someone in a window puts on a shirt. Lo, these ancient forms departing. Newer rites of grace prevail. I have lost Time while gaining it; I am the distances between things.

The nuns minister to me now, thinking I suffer from exhaustion. They try to cover my raw and naked soul with a blanket, and I am reminded of him again: I was thirteen, I had run away, I was vomiting in a bus station somewhere in the middle of the night. He was the only person I could call and he came, gathering me up from the hallway like a bag of bones and placing me gently in the front seat of the car, covering me with a nubby mint-green rug, driving home for hours in the rain. Who could not forgive?

What I know now: Memory is an argument you can't answer. And Life, a dream of Time.

Now I am alone again, except for you, and I thank you for this accident of memory, for the gift of all I could never remember. My life, as you know, has been full of accidents. I was probably born an accident. You are the only recipient of these mysteries, the keeper of all my secrets.

Someday, will I know yours?

All Kindsa People

I was reading a Time/Life book about the Renaissance on my parents' couch when the doorbell rang. It was Aunt Jewel and cousins Snooky and Bobby.

Snooky handed my mom a Baker's Square box: "Banana cream—mmm!" she whispered, winking at me. Bobby was wearing a baseball cap with a patch that read "100% Chicago."

"Hey Shar'!" he wheezed, lighting a cigarette, "how's the Big Apple treatin' ya?"

"Hey kiddo, your father's dyin' ya know," said Aunt Jewel, my dad's oldest sister. She had a fake leather purse in the crook of her arm and a wad of pink Kleenex in the palm of her hand. She pressed the Kleenex into my hand, closed my fingers around it, tapped my fist and said, "You know what to do with that, doncha?" They piled their coats onto Mom's arms and squeezed into the bedroom where Dad was dying from bladder cancer.

"Hiya, Buster!" said Aunt Jewel, lighting a cigarette.

"How ya doin', Frank?" said Snooky.

"Hey hey!" said Bobby. He still looked like Elvis. But not the young sexy Elvis — the drunk Las Vegas Elvis, the fat-and-dead-on-the-toilet Elvis.

Mom was in the kitchen pouring coffee into stoneware cups, cutting the pie, and showing off Dad's "no protein" diet menu. I moved away from the crowd to relax on the plastic-covered couch. The couch had come with the house, recently purchased by my parents, who'd finally moved out of the place my great-grandfather had built four blocks from the Stockyards. The old couple who'd lived in the house before had both died in it.

Bobby lumbered into the living room.

"How's the East Coast there, Shar'? Nice people? What kinda workers are they over there? 'Cause I'm gonna be out there pretty soon."

"Doing what?"

"Workin' on rivers! I been doin' that work for twenty-odd years now. Pourin' concrete for subcontractors, workin' for all kindsa people. I tell ya, Shar', I get along with all kindsa people. In Chicago I drove a furniture delivery truck, and I delivered to all kindsa people. An' I got along with all of 'em 'cause I didn't treat any of 'em any different from the way I would treat you. The way I'm lookin' at you right now, that's the exact way I look at everybody else. I delivered to spics, niggers, A-rabs, Jews, I-talians, and I got along with all of 'em, ya know? I figger, if you're lookin' at people different, then they're gonna sense that and give ya trouble. It's like psychology, ya know? Hey, let's go take a look at your dad. He prob'ly ain't gonna be with us for very long, ya know."

In Dad's bedroom Aunt Jewel was saying, "I got what they call 'severe mental depression.' I'm sick I tell ya—sick! Nobody knows how sick I am. I don't even know how sick I am!"

"How do you like your new place?" Dad whispered. She had just moved into a condominium community for retired people.

"Well, I tell ya, it's a bee-you-tee-full place. It's like a park, ya know—trees, grass, bushes—real nice. But no one there is sociable, ya know what I'm sayin'? You could be layin' dead on the floor for a week and they wouldn't find you. And you have to walk three blocks to get to the street, and I just can't walk. Can't walk! And I sit there all day by myself and think about things I shouldn't be thinking about from 40 years ago, like Lilly's lobotomy and Ma's stomach cancer. I been seein' a psychiatrist that Medicare pays for. I suffered what they call 'trauma' when I moved so soon after my heart attack and my lung collapse. So now I got what they call 'severe mental depression.'"

"You know, I talked to Edna on the phone today," I said. "She's got some kind of incurable bone disease...."

Aunt Jewel threw her hands up and rolled her eyes.

"How come she calls you people and she never calls me? I call everybody in this goddamn family and nobody ever calls me! Nobody gives a damn about me! Nobody knows how sick I am! I don't even know how sick I am!"

"Ah, shut up,Ma, will ya?" Bobby wheezed. "Can'tcha see yer brother's on death's door?"

Snooky and Mom had taken a break from discussing Dad's "no protein diet" at the kitchen table to sit in the living room. Bobby and I joined them. Snooks and Bobby, both in their fifties, were Aunt Jewel's kids from different marriages. Snooky's father was Curly and Bobby's father was Drunkie John. Everyone had liked Curly but then he died. Drunkie John had broken Aunt Jewel's jaw and so when he died nobody cared. *The Godfather* was on TV, the part where Michael is just about to have sex with his young peasant wife on their honeymoon in Italy.

"Hmmm...he's startin' out slow. I like that!" said Snooky, winking at me.

"Hell, I woulda had 'er in bed by now. What's he waitin' for!" rasped Bobby, lighting another cigarette.

"Oh, you two are terrible," said Ma, laughing and flipping her hand. In the bedroom, Dad was saying to Aunt Jewel, "...that's a brand new garage door out there, too. That door's gonna outlast me, that's for sure."

Bon Ami

One sat in Athens. Blue clouds, striped blinds, cigarettes, legs stretched. Saturday was roughing round to a denouement. The sun went in and out.

One's view of the strident Athenian street was compromised occasionally by a pre-existing pathology. Lack of emotion and the fact that one hid behind humor, or whatever, meant nothing as long as one could bathe daily and partake of facials. Additionally, one had become a virgin again: the ancient painful ritual to restore innocence that one had unknowingly submitted to while suffering from dysentery in India had worked, and now, no matter how much one fucked, one was continually reflowered. The process reinforced the whole issue of coming up clean no matter what one suffered unto others for how many countless hours.

One was glad it got windy and the sun went in, as it had always been one's most cherished desire to blot out the sun forever. A single file of carriage horses appeared in the street below, supporting the figure of the elderly gentleman known locally as Bon Ami. Bon Ami alighted lightly and paused in the porch. One placed one's scented handkerchief in one's bosom and descended the staircase. The bell, the calling card placed in the tray, the stepping in politely, the yellow bars of the blinds on the stucco walls all produced a perfect illustration of stasis and malaise.

One made the tea, quickly, and the familiar feeling of an insufficient lunch was upon one. Returning, one found Bon Ami's suit already neatly folded and one's legs already straddling the overturned bureau, the bad champagne and quiet dirty talk in broken English accumulating to a dew point lacking any freshness. One squeezed and squeezed and succeeded in temporarily emasculating Bon Ami. One was paid two thousand dollars American. Everything was outside of time so nothing mattered one way or another except that it was raining again. One knew that as soon as

Bon Ami left one would write a story for the fans back home in which some little girl pees on some old man, thus externalizing the presence that had infected one with its dark fact of demonic possession since the days one was ten years old and tied up in a closet by one's mother while she went out and had a good time on New Year's Eve with some fake cowboy.

One decided to do an interpretative lap dance for Bon Ami, enacting the disappearance of the sun. One kept one eye on the clock and the other on the fingers that stroked one's private parts, Bon Ami's favorite parts. Bon Ami went neither forward nor backward nor moved even incrementally for hours. The phone rang. The sink sweated bullets. The sun came back. One begged Bon Ami to do various things until the impossibility and insipidness of everything finally caught one's annoyance and the lack of affect produced the sensation of a voluptuous sexual politic only possible in Athens. Bon Ami finally satisfied one by acknowledging briefly one's begging by focusing distracted attention on one's secondary sexual characteristics until one came. Afterward, one amused one's self by making a memory dog of various dinnertime triumphs wherein one acted so cruelly one made good friends cry, particularly in small restaurants where other diners would have no choice but to notice. One imagined a similar scenario for the upcoming evening and wondered who one could call because one had already alienated almost everyone.

One's real personality finally made a rare appearance. Having been stored too long in a steamy diner famous for its smell of gin and fried liver, it was occasionally unavailable unto one. Its sudden appearance was always triggered by the long-term effects of the ceremony that restored innocence, causing one's breasts to transmogrify, instigating a pure bodily response that heightened the sunny conditions in the parlor and Bon Ami's attentions. One decided one loved Bon Ami. Thus one allowed Bon Ami to squire one around the agora for a while. However, Bon Ami had no way of knowing that anything of significance was happening, as everything was happening underneath understanding, and that, one knew, was the crux of all one's problems with others: the ability of the general public to intuit what was going on in one's psyche was severely limited. Like rugs or doves or vases, one was always The Eternally Observed and people like Bon Ami The Eternal Observers, and that was how the whole thing always worked itself out, although sometimes there were problems when people like Bon Ami got the roles confused, and so it was one's duty to keep the status quo going for one's own protection.

One decided to put on the characteristic petulance guaranteed to move things along. One knew that every single particular had to be jiggled toward the Bon Ami event passing and becoming history. Bon Ami was so bold as to make inquiries regarding where to meet next. In God, one sneered. I am yours in Christ, Bon Ami said in all seriousness, but on the earthly plane, like a lobster in exile in a tank full of other lobsters in a grocery store. Whatever, one countered. One didn't give a flying goddamn.

Tomorrow

for Barbara Rothman

The air was pleasantly gold and I felt good. Marie was crumpled up like a rag doll on the grass, skirt raised, no panties, exposed. I was keen on her in those days even though I didn't try to prevent Cardona's hands from scrying her. Still, it was only the first morning, a Saturday, and I had my Saturdays and Sundays off and had been going to bed early and sleeping for twelve hours straight: quite like old times — a day's holiday and back to work after. That nothing came of it except me being witness to their flagrant animalizing was certainly not my fault. Sickened, I suggested we raft.

After a half hour dozing on the raft my mind was lulled and I didn't think of anything. Upon waking, however, I found the two of them all crisscrossed, his nose burrowed deep in her upper reaches. Back on land we got off the raft: Marie all helpless, her wet white blooms mixed with my own little thrill of pleasure when we finally got to the parking lot where I knew I would have her later, or at least someday, maybe even tomorrow, and it would be on top of her mother, the famous escape artist whose last escape, unfortunately, had failed, and now she lay buried in a glass-topped coffin under the parking lot where she'd been buried alive under klieg lights for a week until she died. I let my hand gloss across the glass-topped coffin. I let it stay. I let my head sink down upon it. Then I let my hand nonchalantly fall onto Marie's knee, perpendicular to the saintly face of her mother. She didn't seem to mind, so while Cardona was off behind some cars peeing I let my fingers spread out across her lap like quaint villagers picking through trinkets in a street market. Of course, I couldn't expect someone as dumb as Marie to see my point, so when she turned away I took it as my cue to delve deeper into the mystery. I saw then why my employer, Cardona, liked her so much: her upturned eyes all blue, forming a smooth swimming pool. I pictured those eyes lighting some greasy back street, or a department store parking lot bereft of cars after midnight with nobody around and the trains going by, where I would climb onto Marie as onto that raft, her tawny red-earth hair falling gently over gravel. She could even drive the car if she desired, though the way I pictured it was with her hands working the pedals and her legs spread across the top of the seat and me working her from behind as we crashed into a lamp post and the bulb burst and light cascaded all around us like the collision of Venus and Jupiter.

When the sun got too hot for standing around, and I whined that we should leave, Cardona, suddenly and from a great distance, dived like a rogue streetcar onto Marie, and kept diving and diving and pattering about typists and fingers that dance, and then kept diving some more. I asked him for two days off during the week but he was too busy diving to answer. So there I was, alone under the sun, getting too warm, and suddenly I began to remember how Cardona did me like that once : I was shorter then, my feet could hardly reach the Dictaphone pedal, and we laughed about that as he stood behind me, rubbing my shoulders.

"It's the holidays," he said, "everybody's rubbing somebody's shoulders."

Half-jokingly, I had suggested that a swim might do, so down to the harbor we went. We rode the ferry all day long, feeding each other strawberries. I demonstrated what being a drum majorette meant. He did his gorilla impersonation while watching my ass. When the ferry stopped running we found a ditch and made it. Then, under cover of night, back to the office to make it again, under some overturned furniture. But now, today, he had Marie flat on the floor of the parking lot and my stomach was turning and I was wondering: if not today and not yesterday then when? Tomorrow?

The Empty Quarter

"Amid the world's expanse . . . is the cold spring of oblivion"
— *Pushkin*

I met you in a gallery on a national holiday. You were standing in front of a sculpture entitled, "Jesus the Lizard of Old Borneo." You had pale hair and pocky skin, fingernails bitten so low bonnets of flesh curved heavily over them. You walked over to a folding chair & sat down, twirling your ragged bangs with your thumb and first finger. You sat head bowed and squirming, twirling your hair, chin down so low it touched your chest. You were stasis and malaise, safely elusive; passivity at a fever pitch. Then you read your poetry. A small crowd gathered around, and I could hear the whispered comparisons of you to famous dead French writers with bad complexions. You were a one-man literary history show, everyone there was loving it, approaching you like a sacred shrine, their own fragile egos in hand as offerings. The packing house heiress, observing you from across the room, told those in attendance, "Genius doesn't have to do anything. People will hover around it like doves." I was with a big clean Catholic boy from a pure and distant suburb, and he hung heavily next to me, listening to you discuss your newest pseudonym. The big clean Catholic boy was mad at me for refusing to get a perm and wear dresses. He wanted me to be the type of girl he didn't have to explain to his parents when we went to their house on Oriole Avenue for Easter. I wanted to be the type of girl people like his parents hated. I was South Side skinny, just old enough to vote, wearing black pants two sizes too small, drinking brandy from a flask like a writer. As we were leaving I said good-bye to you, and you didn't answer me; such was the weight of your intelligence. Later, on the crowded subway train, some guy grabbed me between my legs and ran out the door as it closed. When I told the Catholic boy about it he moved to the middle of the car, sputtering a quick "Shut up!" Back at his apartment he beat me up and pulled the phone off the wall. After he fell asleep I took $20 from his wallet for a cab home, and once I got home wrote about it in my journal while soaking in a Calgon bubble bath.

One year later you and me were talking by the cigarette machine, after a benefit lecture at the university. I told you how big Catholic boy had left me after I got too worried about being pregnant, but then miscarried early when I got up to switch the tv channel. I squatted down and then passed out. I woke up on his bed with clots of blood in my underwear. He said, "You get too hysterical. You eat too much sugar." I thought, someday this'll all be great literature. You listened, head bowed, without looking at me. You invited me to a party at the gallery that was currently showing your sculptures of men's bodies with horses' heads on them. You called your show "Bloomingdale's Store For Men." I said I'd try and make it, but instead went to New York with Davey, the BonTon baker. I was attracted to the plaintive romance of his bare brown mattress, lack of bathroom, his smell like old clothes, the shooting gallery games in his kitchen, and the cinematic aspect of yelling Puerto Rican mothers two floors down waking us up after a night of love. I was attracted to anything unlike the big clean Catholic boy. We fucked once in the morning & he tied me up. Afterwards we had breakfast at the White Castle & went shopping at the Salvation Army for paisley pants. Afterwards we left for New York for a week. But Davey ended badly when the big boy came back, saying he'd been through therapy successfully. Davey still loved me, and paid for my psychiatrist after the big boy threw a chair at me upstairs at the beatnik reunion reading. I gave Davey my rare 45 of "La Vie En Rose" when I left him again. I thought it was a nice gesture for my autobiography.

Two years after Davey I was still thinking about him. I was thinking about him one night at the Step-Hi Lounge when Deborah, Constance and me were brainstorming our new revolutionary literary magazine. We were writers and college graduates, staying out late and wearing black. We were reading *Pride and Prejudice* and *Journey to the End of Night*. We were writing about bourgeois kitchens and death. Deborah's boyfriend, the anonymous artist in a long black coat, was your best friend. When he came to pick her up he reported to us what you were working on at the moment, something called "A Story of Bucktown," in which you wake up at 7 a.m. and go to the 7-11 for orange pop and hear the Vienna Boys Choir in the cooler. He said it was so great it was going to be the liner notes for an album by a new band whose name was "aluminum foil" spelt backwards, the spoken soundtrack for a black and white movie about Bucktown, and the basis of an experimental play about nuns. He said you were trying to pare down your life to the bare essentials required for literature: generic pork and beans from a can, black clothes and a bad attitude. I pictured your pale head tossing through nightmares on your dirty pillow, your poor apartment smelling of borscht, unwashed underwear and hair. I thought, what great things you'd be writing if you fell in love with me.

I was living with a nice guy who owned things and knew how to carry a briefcase to maximum effect, even though the only things in it were his cigarettes. He made things comfy. He made cashew chicken in the wok and watched public television cooking shows. We really ate a lot. I was writing poems about girls named Nada who fell in the middle of freeways, and girls named Indigo who bowled in league night candle-lights at the Miami Bowl. The nice guy really took care of me, but I felt things were getting too easy. One early Sunday morning I was lying in the living room, staring at the radiator in the corner by the window, listening to Edith Piaf's "C'est Hambourg," which always brought on thoughts of eternity. I never could write about eternity, just girls waving from chop suey restaurants. I put on an insufficient jacket and walked down Wilson Street towards Bucktown, the place you had written about in your story, the place where the hillbillies lived. It was cold and the dry autumn leaves were scraping the sidewalk softly. I could see the beginnings of breakfasts through the slightly open curtains of the big houses' bay windows. This was the kind of weather, and the time of day, I liked best, because it reminded me of when I began writing on autumn mornings my first year in high school. Underneath the elevated train at Broadway some old guy said, "Hey honey, wanna make a few bucks?" When I said yeah he couldn't believe it and said, "Yeah? Are you alright or something?" I said let's just hurry up. We walked into the Wilson Men's Shelter, and the old men slouching in the lobby looked up from their dirty gray chests. He lived in room 205 and his name was Bridge. Inside his room there was a feeling of Formica and cigarettes. He was nervous and said, "I don't know, can you just masturbate for me? I can't really screw girls anymore. Well, at least you know I won't hurt you." His mattress was soft and smelled like shit. He stood at the edge of the bed and didn't even take his clothes off. He came in his pants and then I left. I used the $25 he gave me to buy the nice guy and me breakfast at the German pastry shop, a ticket to the movies, and beers at the Greek taverna. But over beers at the Greek taverna, I knew what I had to do; I had to be with you.

That Saturday I was shopping at Kroch's and Brentano's for bargain books. Your girlfriend was living in Fez and the nice guy I was living with was out of town. I called you on the public phone and asked if you wanted to meet later at the Get Me High Lounge. You said yes; I ran home to take a moisturizing bath. At the Get Me High I was wearing blue plaid pants, a big black sweater and no underwear. I brought a poem I had written about you. You brought your manuscript. You smelled like an unwashed winter cap. Some people were reading their bad poetry on stage. A big blonde girl was reciting a poem about working for the circus. A little bald guy walked up on stage behind her and pretended to pick bugs out of her big blonde hair. The woman next to me got nauseous and passed out along the bar. Butchie the cook got into a fight and someone called the cops. Some Hawaiian guys came in arguing about their golfing scores. By then it was 2 a.m. and I'd read your whole manuscript, *Lost Dog On A Dirty Beach*. It made me want to fuck you in a church. I told you I wanted to have an affair with you. You kept talking about wild Zarathustras so I hit the side of your head and said it again. You were silent and looked me in the eyes. We walked back to your room at the Norman Hotel, across the street from Wrigley Field, two blocks from the Wilson Men's Shelter, and I was hoping I'd see Bridge so you would like me better. We walked seven flights up the bad stairs to your room. Papers full of poems were thrown so thickly on your floor there was no carpet showing through. Your bed did smell like borscht. Your pillow was a bunched up robe and your sheet was a sleeping bag with a hole in it where the feathers fell out. A roach crawled across my foot. You fucked me up the ass and when I turned around to watch you your head was thrown back and your mouth was open. Afterwards I cut my lip on some weird bone sticking out of your chest and you smiled at me naked like some old hillbilly. You said, "I never thought I'd be with someone as beautiful as you." I knew that soon I'd leave the nice guy I was living with and my writing would improve. I showed you the poem I wrote about you. You said, "I don't really like the first part."

The nice guy I was living with kicked me out. I moved to a room downstairs from you, where I could hear Harry Carey singing "Take Me Out To The Ball Game" every day at about 3. There was a roach nest behind the kitchen shelves, old linoleum that couldn't be cleaned, even with bleach, a broken bed and a dresser that smelled of sick. I shared a bathroom down the hall with a middle-aged Mexican man who smoked fat Havanas and spit up a lot, thick yellow with grains, in the bathtub near the drain. The landlord was a big yuppie who greased his chest when he trimmed the hedges. I worked and you didn't. I wondered where you got your money. Every day I came home from work at 5 and the fans were getting drunk because the Cubs had lost again. To avoid them I walked through the alley under the El. You were sleeping after writing all day.

Your key was above the door. I came in and half-asleep you said, "Who won, the pots or the pans?" The light through the broken blue shade coated us in a blue hour, and like a rare silver bell I was resonant with dreams of drowning and death. You got up and went back to writing. I went downstairs and typed letters till late at night, hoping you could hear my typewriter. I wrote to Constance who had just ended her friendship with me. I apologized profusely, for what I didn't really know. I told her I felt exiled from comfort. I couldn't sleep so I started reading a book about Arabia.

My scope of living was narrowing and there was nothing much to write about, but I enjoyed reading about Arabia, especially the desert called the Empty Quarter. We were living to your rhythm: restaurants were bourgeois, dancing was useless, eating was an extravagance, friends were a waste of time, conversation cut into precious writing time. Everyone in town knew you were the one, the one who really knew, and you had to maintain your image. At Elena's, the cheapest Mexican restaurant in Wicker Park, your acolytes had gathered after your Valentine's Day reading at The Black Cat Club. The packing house heiress leaned over the jalapeño bowl and said to me, "You're so lucky you get to sleep with him. What does he fuck like?" The local literary entrepreneur, who couldn't work because his eyes hurt, asked me as he passed me en route to the bathroom, "So what's he really like—at home, I mean?" You squirmed your discomfort at being in a restaurant, and everyone knew that was the cool thing to do. So they stared at you and asked about the diatribal articles you were writing for local magazines that made fun of the writers we knew, most of them my former friends. Your lines were quoted back breathlessly as if you weren't in the room, by your best friend, the anonymous artist in a long black coat. "Hey," he said, "'the common man shops for status at Sears.'" And the people agreed, their admiration shining through. You rolled your pale blue eyes, made a long face, twirled a few strands of your ragged bangs between your first finger and thumb, head down. It was the cool thing to do. On the way out of the restaurant, the local literary entrepreneur asked me, "So when did you start writing? After you guys started going out?" "No," I said, "I started writing ten years ago." Back at home I took a bubble bath and read more about the Empty Quarter. I wondered about what would happen if someone were brought to live there. I imagined having the ability to act out any heinous crime there, to perform any drama, to exert any power. The possibilities of emptiness seemed endless. I thought maybe I could write about it.

I was much tougher now, and my writing was tougher too. I was writing about knives and throats, shattered clavicles and ghouls of love, the cud of ardor, bare void bones, and the moon my head gorged on the starry gas of love. I was so tough everyone at work hated me. I brought my Arabia books to work with me and read them at my desk. My boss wanted to fire me, so he wrote me up. I told you all about it. I figured you'd see how tough I was. You nodded and said, "Hmmm." I got mad but then I stopped. What need did one have of those things which didn't contribute directly to literature, or the image of literature, like comfort, support, security and love? We all needed it tough if we didn't kid ourselves much. My childhood poverty couldn't be helped, and what respite could I expect? After all, you'd been poor too, playing in the ditch at Frog Hollow, your friend who knew the white trash of Indiana had said. But a visit to your parents' house confused me. I took the last ten dollars I had till payday, which was three days away, to buy the train ticket. Your rhythm of living suggested I should've stayed home and written, or read some small obscure books of subversive critical theory by well-fed middle-aged Frenchmen living in Lyons. It was a grim two-hour trajectory from the West Side city poverty to the northern suburbs' insulated wealth, to the doorstep of the ranch house on Trillium Court, to the big living room and its many niceties. You slunk cross-kneed and head down, making long disgusted mouths, into a corner of the John M. Smyth couch like a physical cripple, and didn't move. Your parents moved pleasant and well-fed through the rooms, cajoling you into speech. You twirled strands of your ragged bangs between your thumb and first finger and mumbled responses to their well-tempered questions. Coming back from the bathroom I heard talk of stocks and bonds. On the train back I asked if you owned stocks, and you said, "Some." Later I asked where Frog Hollow and the white trash of Indiana fit in. You said, "I just played with them."

Living became different then. When I came home from work every afternoon at about 2 I could hear Jon in 25 playing the viola, and Steve in 13 playing his piano. It was cool and dark in my apartment and I loved to listen to the music and be still. Then the sound of pounding from upstairs would intrude. It meant that you were writing and I wasn't. But things had changed. I didn't care about writing anymore, though once I snuck upstairs when you weren't there, to see what you were writing—a three-page poem about Christ the fish that proved again you were a genius. I knew my writing didn't matter anymore. So I worked, slept and read about Arabia, especially the Empty Quarter. I imagined the possibilities. The need to escape and the desire to stay. I pictured a man and a woman there, who inspire in each other the most destructive acts of nature, because the sameness of the landscape allows it. I imagined actually feeling the emptiness, being brought to the edge of emptiness by one's own fears, and then being forced to conquer them in order to stay alive. I imagined the man fucking the woman in the Wadi Dawasir, the mysterious desert river, fucking her from behind and submerging her head in the water for a long time as he comes. I imagined him asking her to hold a knife to his chest as he fucks her on top, so that the closer he comes to climax, the deeper the point of the knife goes. I imagined the maddening panorama of barrenness, and the need to fill it up, and the need to escape the possibilities. After sex one day you said, "I'm planning on going to Paris. Do you think you wanna meet me there?" As always, you nobly asked no consideration and gave none in return. I worked every day for three months to meet you there.

That first day we fucked on the floor of your friend Frances' apartment on the Avenue du Maine. It was an illegal sublet and the farina-faced concierge gave me dirty looks when she saw me go up and down the stairs. In the mornings I bought baguettes, pâté, and sterilized milk. During the afternoons I went to the Montparnasse cemetery to write letters. Evenings I made couscous and listened to the radio while you typed in the other room. Everything about Paris was beautiful. I thought, "Here, I could begin to write again." So I did. I showed you a poem. You said, "I like everything but the last part." I said, "So what else?" You said, "Whaddya mean what else?" I put the poem away. It didn't seem good enough to work on now. So we saw Baudelaire's grave in the rain. I spoke to a cat sitting on Colette's headstone. I removed the ugly plastic flowers from Sartre's new tomb. We ate hot dogs with mustard in the Marais. Young prostitutes danced behind a Plexiglas window on the Boulevard Montmartre. We did a reading together at Shakespeare & Co. Everyone listened to you with rapt attention and laughter and left during my set. I got drunk and yelled all along the Boulevard Saint Jacques. I threw my folder full of poems into the gutter and Frances fished them out. After that we split up. You moved to the Hotel Stella, on the Rue des Trois Freres, at the top of Montmartre; I moved to the Hotel Ma Caravan, on the Boulevard Clichy. Fat Maurice the desk clerk had a scar on his neck where a goiter'd been removed. I drank warm red wine with cripples and midgets in the bar downstairs that stank of urine. I ate saucisses and merguez with the Arabs who ran the peep shows. They jokingly offered me a job and when I turned it down they said, "Your tits are too small anyway." Then our friend China Tartarini, the performance artist, came to visit with her friend Facetia Torrestico, the Puerto Rican beauty. Facetia wore polka dot pants, lime green mini-skirts, leather bustiers and sat all day in cafés. She was so beautiful the French spoke English to her. China performed at Le Pensée Sauvage and Facetia came along.

Afterwards we all went to the Café of the Jumping Dog, and I fell in love with Facetia. I stayed at the cafe late, till everybody left, and the jumping dog jumped. Then I said to Facetia, "Can we go somewhere together?" She laughed at me and got up to leave, but I stayed seated. At the door she turned and said, "Well? Didn't you want to go somewhere?" She lived in our old arondissment, on the Rue Froideaux, the road of cold waters, that ran for a time through the cemetery. We walked together there in silence. She had a nice apartment with a bathroom and real wood floors that some man was paying for. She had expensive perfumes in blue bottles in her bathroom. She had a mirrored marble shower with spigots all around. She took a long shower and had me rub some kind of cream all over her. She closed her eyes and opened her mouth. She acted like I wasn't there. She acted like a photograph and I didn't like that. She slipped into bed and went to sleep. Lying next to her all night long, I thought about all the things that were wrong with me, and the idea of the Empty Quarter. I left at 6 a.m. and it was raining. I was in her courtyard, almost to the gate, when she ran out naked and laughed at me.

I saw you again on New Year's Eve, at the apartment of three Senegalese students. Out the window the Eiffel Tower was glowing from its green laser beams. You said, "Do you want to go home with me?" In your room you spit on your palm and rubbed the saliva on your cock. I said, "I don't like getting fucked up the ass." You said, "You're just not adventurous." I said, "Tell me your fantasies." You said, "I don't have any." I invented some elaborate fantasies that I thought would arouse you. Then, you said, "Hmmm. But you still won't do what I want to do." I said, "When you fuck me up the ass you're rejecting me, as a girl." You said, "You're talking crazy again." I didn't love you anymore, but I couldn't give up because it would mean I wasn't tough enough. One day we met for sandwiches in the Tuileries and I told you I'd finally decided to give up writing. You said, "Didn't you decide that once before?" There was a long silence as I watched a black dog bite a little boy's hand. You said, "Do you want to go with me to India?" I said yeah.

My first day in Bombay a big brown roach flew into my face. We ate *thali* meals on banana leaves. I threw up, had diarrhea, sneezed and cried. We took an overnight boat on the Arabian Sea. On the beach in Panjim we drank ice cold beers under a bamboo awning and peed next to poisonous frogs. We fucked on the beach at night and the sparking sand made stars behind my head. I had sunstroke on the 18-hour bus to Bangalore. I was sick for two days but we were on a schedule so I got out of bed to walk to the temple, the palace, the big bull sculpture. In Calcutta I had this dream: the rickshaw we're riding in changes to a horse carriage that takes us through British India. A young girl who looks a little like Facetia Torrestico is running towards the carriage, taunting me. I say, "Don't worry, I won't come after you." She comes closer and closer, and finally with an air of tragic urgency says, "I'm so beautiful!" I pull off all her clothes. She disintegrates into small pale fruits which I pick up and throw into the air. They turn into flower petals and slowly drift down. The sky ripples to royal blue, the crescent moon appears, I throw an apricot into the air and the sky turns amber. We woke up and left for Darjeeling. We stayed in a lodge on a hill with a view of the clouds lifting over the Himalayas every morning. When it got dark the stars and the little lights from houses across the valley made the landscape seem like one big sky. One night I tried to initiate sex with you but got the impression that my body disgusted you. You winced slightly and turned away. I remembered when I first met you at the gallery on a national holiday you were reading your poems that described women's bodies less than lovingly: "her teeth were bad and she smelled like rankling flesh," "her skin fell to wattles, her floral breath turned to rank gas," "she sucked just a little more life from my pious, anxious bones." I was confident then that you didn't think of me like that. But now I felt what made me a girl also made me soft and exploitable, fat, progenitive and bovine. I began to think how much better it was to be a boy, to be hard and cold, diffident, distant and hateful. The further we traveled into the country the more we hated each other. We each became our worst selves, and I began to see the landscape as the central character in the drama. I began thinking of the Empty Quarter. We crossed the border into Nepal and bought Coca-Cola. On the night bus to Katmandu fireflies were brilliant in the forests. The roosters in cages on the top of the bus crowed when the sun came up. In Ghorepani I went to the outhouse at 3 a.m. and saw seven Himalayan peaks under a huge moon, the Big Dipper spread out across the sky. In Varanasi we saw the Ganges in a golden morning light. In Udaipur I had sunstroke again and amoebic dysentery. I had one slice of toast and a cup of tea three times a day, while you left early to see the city. One day I peeked into your journal and saw what you had been writing about me. You characterized me as weak and needy, missing mother, therapist and friends. I saw myself picked apart like a vivisection: "she can't write, gets mad and then gives up," "she has few ideas of her own," "she is controlled by her emotions," "she's not sure of her own point of view." But I knew it was true. I now weighed ninety-seven pounds and didn't have the strength to fight. I had no idea what action to take, but wanted to stay and prove you wrong; for my own peace of mind I had to. I thought, this is what the Empty Quarter can do to you, and I started to describe my characters in my diary.

Back in Chicago we found an apartment across from a halfway house. You said you could see yourself living there and liking it. You were moving artistically in that direction. You began to develop your public persona by hanging out in hillbilly bars. Your parents took us to upscale Thai restaurants and paid the bills with their credit cards. My parents took us to diners in search of the perfect meat loaf. My father had cancer, but no one knew it yet but him. My sister had abandoned her two-year-old son to live with a Puerto Rican drug dealer and his mother. Our writer friends Carlos and Cynthia asked if I could take them to the

Stockyards neighborhood where I'd grown up. They wanted to see my father, a butcher. They'd never seen a butcher before. I showed them the abandoned factories and packing houses, St. John of God Church, Ashland Avenue and St. Joseph High School. I told them, "These are the things that made me write. These are the things I wanted to tell about. The old Poles and Mexicans in their big plaid pants shopping at Goldblatt's, Dad's old butcher shop with the sawdust on the floor, his lime-green Rambler, waving to trains full of livestock while stopped at the red light at 47th Street, how the summer smell of the Stockyards was so bad my mother wouldn't let us go out and play 'cause we'd bring it in on our clothes, and we had no air conditioning, just a window fan in the kitchen 'cause we were poor, and the day Toni, my adopted sister, an American Indian, first came to visit and I taught her how to print her name with a red, white and blue American Airlines pen, and we ate vanilla ice cream at the bottom of the stairs, talking to Grandma while Mom and Dad spoke with the social worker in the kitchen, and Georgie Kowalski, my best friend, talking about sex in the sewing room at school, making out behind the bowling alley with the Puerto Rican pinball king, and my other best friend Norma Olvera, who lived on Paulina Street, where I'd go on Saturdays, and her mother would make black bean tortillas and call me 'weta,' then she married Leo Castillo and I was maid of honor, and after the wedding we went to McDonald's, and now her brother Henry has AIDS...I just wanted to tell people what life was like here." Carlos said, "This doesn't seem like the type of place where you'd grow up. You seem like you come from the suburbs." He thought instead you were the one who fit right in. It occurred to me that you had somehow appropriated my past for your public package, and whether that was true or not it made me mad. "Now," Carlos said to me, "I guess I should take you seriously." It occurred to me to leave the city.

In August we drove to Brooklyn. My last night in Chicago I dreamt I was singing, "Open The Kingdom." I got a job teaching freshman comp at the college and you were unemployed. It didn't matter to you when there was no food in the house, but to me it meant I hadn't risen above my old circumstances yet. I made new friends and began writing again. Every night we watched "The Honeymooners" together and fell asleep. We stopped having sex, but I still needed affection. I had an affair with a freshman from Flatbush. We fucked for the first time in his Toyota under the Verrazano Bridge because he lived with his parents and they were Catholic. There were lots of other cars there. They were the regulars. Some had sheets strung up to cover their windows so that no one could see inside. Some were blasting soft romantic music. One couple pulled up and ate a nice Chinese take-out dinner before they fucked. Another couple drove up in a big black van with a dark hairy devil fucking a fat white girl painted on both sides. They were playing Barry White and the Love Unlimited Orchestra. When they were done they got out and walked around. The girl, wearing a blue tube top and tight stonewashed jeans that emphasized her bloat, closed her eyes and lifted her arms languidly, as if conducting an invisible symphony. The guy got out a soft cloth and rubbed an invisible smudge off the devil's powerful thigh. The freshman unbuttoned my shirt and began rubbing my breasts. He said, "You like that, don't you?" He took his shirt off I saw his big baby belly. When he lowered himself onto me the big baby belly came first. We tried to fuck but every time he put it in he got soft. He said it had to do with being Catholic and living at home. I told him to take me home. On the BQE we pulled over so he could masturbate. A month later a big pink and white man in my class asked if I liked to see plays and I said yeah. We saw *The Father* by Strindberg, and I liked the line, "You must know how maddening it is to have your most ardent desires thwarted and your will restrained." We went for café au lait at the Cloisters. He said he was obsessed with me. He said, "I saw you last week on the Lower East Side." He said, "I saw you walking around and you got me aroused." He said, "You got me aroused and I wanted to screw you. You got me aroused and I wanted to rape you." The dry white skin on his hard pink face was flaking in the soft white and yellow light of the fake stained glass windows. I thought maybe he had eczema. He looked about sixty-five. He said, "Excuse me for being so raucous. I'm a bit wild and woolly at times. I haven't been able to be with people for the last ten years, for reasons I can't go into in public." He said, "Women today are fabulous. I'm sure your mother never put a personal ad in the *Village Voice*." He wanted to take me to his apartment in Sheepshead Bay to show me his collection of letters from Otto Rank. I said I wasn't interested. He said, "Then why were you smiling at me on the R train the other day? Why were you acting so coquettish in class? You know, I caught the eye of at least a hundred women in Bloomingdale's yesterday. You know, my brother was mentioned by Levi-Strauss." I said again I wasn't interested. He said, "You know I could do damage to you. I'm a big man and you're just a girl." I said, "Go ahead." Then I left. I went home alone, took a bubble bath and wrote it all down. Then I curled my legs up under me and went to sleep. The next morning you hadn't even noticed I'd gotten in late. That summer you went to California for a month to think. Once a week you called collect to say you loved me. I was working at a high-priced natural make-up store on the Upper East Side. My boss was a teenage girl from New Jersey who lived with her father the oil mogul. Every day the puffy-eyed uptown widows wearing pancake make-up would come in and abuse me. The older ones looked like used Q-tips. Every day I took a small piece of merchandise home with me. The day you returned I bought Chinese shoes and registered for classes. That evening we were watching a PBS special on schizophrenia. A disheveled young man tried to kill his father and then said, "Even these walls have headaches." During the commercial you said you were leaving. I asked you why. You said, "I'm just not happy anymore. I want love, support, and peace of mind." I said, "Is there anything I can do to make you stay?" You said no.

Then it was nighttime December and it was my birthday. I was wearing a short red coat, walking alone on Avenue A and it was raining. I was walking fast 'cause it was freezing. You met me at the Ukrainian bar. You gave me an angel card, a plastic baby and a wiggle picture of the Shroud of Turin. We went to Pyramid for happy hour. A heavy metal band was setting up and we argued about deconstruction. You said your new interest was the pornography industry as metaphor. You bought me drinks till you were broke so I bought you tacos with my new credit card. I had just gotten published in a downtown magazine, and you said, "Gee, you're getting famous." I thought I was still in love with you. The next night at a reading someone told me you were dating an androgynous Canadian performance artist who worked weekdays in the Peep Show and weekends describing her clitoris in clinical terms, that was her performance. Later that month I saw you drunk at a Lower East Side New Year's Eve party. I wore a long red scarf tied around my head and you tried to be friendly. I said, "I think your new relationship's a travesty." Later I apologized and you pressed my forehead with your index finger and looked me in the eyes and I started to cry. That night I decided to write "The Empty Quarter" differently, more honestly, by changing the false plot constructs of the original fiction to a structure based mostly on reality, though some of the scenes were drawn more colorfully, and some hadn't happened at all. I understood more clearly now the metaphor of emptiness. It was difficult at first because I didn't want to contribute further to your celebrity back home, but I also realized that repression had been born in the maintenance of certain images, such as your false public persona, and the falseness of my own in response to it. When I finished I felt as if you were gone from me, that the last ten years, beginning with the big clean Catholic boy, had finally ended, and I was glad. It was 1990. The fascist Republicans were still in power, but Nelson Mandela was free. A few weeks later a friend introduced me to a boy I liked who made me dinner and gave me a Shiva figure. We went to a party in Manhattan's tiniest apartment and you were there. You passed him the yellow flower someone had just given you. He thanked you, put it in his sweater.